RAVENNA GETS

OTHER BOOKS BY TONY BURGESS

Pontypool Changes Everything

Caesarea

The Hellmouths of Bewdley

Fiction for Lovers

Ravenna Gets

Tony Burgess

ANVIL PRESS | VANCOUVER

Anvil Press Publishers Inc.
P.O. Box 3008, Main Post Office
Vancouver, B.C. V6B 3X5 CANADA
www.anvilpress.com

Library and Archives Canada Cataloguing in Publication is available.
ISBN: 978-1-897535-32-5

Printed and bound in Canada
Cover design by Mutasis Creative
Interior design by HeimatHouse

Represented in Canada by the Literary Press Group
Distributed by the University of Toronto Press

The publisher gratefully acknowledges the financial assistance of the Canada Council for the Arts, the Canada Book Fund, and the Province of British Columbia through the B.C. Arts Council and the Book Publishing Tax Credit.

FOR
DEREK MCCORMACK

Main Street

Captain Crunch is sitting at the Golden Orchard. The waitress watches him, her only customer, sitting in the orange wooden booth. She is waiting for him to finish his draft. Outside, snow is driving the pickup trucks back. Through the front window of the Golden Orchard, beyond the flash-fire of the waitress's face, two colours streak through the snow—blue and red. Blue is the background and red is the letters. L maybe, and the Empire consonant. Small o and, even smaller, a one-legged a. The snow falls here every day. The Lite-Brite wall that hangs over the edge of the bay sprays snow and ice from November to April, even when the sky is blue. The people in town grow accustomed to it, being heavy, being blind in unexpected places —near Coolz Own Video store, their arms and legs as comfortable as giant wheels, rolling and seizing in the act of giving way.

Captain Crunch has his own tractor with a back-mounted blower. When he's finished his drink he'll head back out and resume removing snow. From Main Street, along the south side, past the hexagonal United Church and up to the retirement condos, behind the used computer store with sails of paper print in the window, hundreds of huge numbers consisting of thousands of tiny ones, then three antique stores in a row, tea cups and mousetraps, some full of tea, some full of mice, and the chocolatier with candy as big as big babies, and the pizzeria, a bald man at an oven. All the things on Main Street you expect, with alleyways and brown standards and a few people who ignore things as they grow snow parts and walk in a flitting grey light.

Captain Crunch lines up his tractor so the blower's teeth are pressed into a wall of new snow beside the church. He brings a purple hand up to his cleft upper lip and pulls cold spit away from the imperfect seal of his closed mouth. He breathes in hard from his nose, hoping to vacuum out the base of his throat. He throws the switch that starts the blower. Coins blur in a tin lid tilted back against plexiglas.

Barb watches Captain Crunch from across the street. She is placing a Christmas cone by the ankle of a wool dog. She has trouble seeing because she has decorated the inside of her clothing store with spray-on snow. She watches the blue light on Captain Crunch's tractor.

"It's a Rottie."

"What?"

Barb pulls herself out carefully to keep her tall hair away from the rigid fingers of the mannequin and looks back over her shoulder.

"Rottie. There's too many big dogs loose in this town."

The little man who just spoke lays socks on glass, then touches his neat white hair once with two fingers.

"It's eating a banana frozen to the grate."

Barb sighs and returns to the mannequin. Naked. The front of the church, if she could see it, would sit below the upward curve of the breast. Captain Crunch's blue light would have lit for a moment where the nipple should be. The blue light is gone.

"Harry Croce is going to back out of that alley and get run over by a truck."

She strikes a pose not unlike the mannequins. Hands free of the body with the head swung up over the left shoulder. Both bodies graceful and alert.

The little man marks down the socks by fifty per cent.

"He is so."

The blower is shredding the alley.

19 Pine Street

Leo's mother Gloria is watching TV. The living room, a dust world of shiny glass beads, is in disarray. The only couch cushion still in the couch is wrapping Gloria's hips and the rest, the couch cushions, the chair cushions, the pillows and throws are all arranged, as if pulled by the draw of something draining down through the floor, in a circular wall around Leo, who is curled up and sleeping. He's only been asleep for two hours. The night was long and terrible. Leo bucking his legs and twisting backward, covered in the light grease of a child's high fever. Crying out through sequined lips and shivering in rocket-ship pyjamas. He has been sick like this, on and off, for weeks. Gloria doesn't like this phrase, *he's been sick for weeks.* She has heard it and used it herself so often recently. She remembers when it was *he's been like this for days* and now she fears she will have to say *he's been sick for months.* So she practises, braces herself for when it becomes true by saying it *seems* like he's been sick for months. After that, he will probably always have been sick.

Will the illness push back time? she wonders. Will it soon include her own queasy first weeks of pregnancy? Maybe it is an unlimited thing. Maybe she herself, the mother stopping ahead to protect faces from furniture, is nothing more than a condition, a term of disease, a sleeping shape, like a bowling pin, or a night owl, sitting behind the shadow of a door or on the thin tip of a tree, so narrow and sharp, always meant to do this, to enter the child who was supposed to leave her easily. A child on the floor. Gloria leans

over Leo and sniffs the air above him. He smells like a man does. Composting children smell like men. Leo coughs. His hand comes up and touches his eyelids.

That's right. He was a hockey player. This was the same gesture he used to wipe sweat from his face on the rink. A muscled blond boy with emerald eyes. Fast as a spider. He always stole the other mothers' hearts.

Leo coughs and sits up in his blue tea cup.

"How you feelin'?"

Leo doesn't answer. He's pulling his jaw down to open his face.

"Want some juice?"

Leo blinks and looks at the TV. An airplane is shot down over the Ukraine.

Gloria stands up, turns and plumps her lone couch cushion. She walks over to the window and draws back the blinds. A large horrible ship of sunlight capsizes against the back wall. Dead shadows are pushed into the carpet by the new dead who burn in bright pain.

Leo, her first-born son, a broken egg on the floor, has fallen back asleep.

"Hi. Brenda."

Gloria pops another Nicorette.

"Yeah. I've been chewing these things for fuckin' five years."

The light cuts into Leo's shoulder. It pulls at the bristles on Gloria's shin.

"You know what I think, B. I think he's got…I don't know really, but, I saw this thing about West Nile virus and…"

Gloria shelters her eyes. She listens and feels her whole mind wet with the act of speculation.

"Well, I'm just trying to think outside. Doctors, you know what I realize about doctors?"

Leo's back is rising into the light. A turtle boy with a margarine shell. He slips back down, cold and gone.

"They don't know what they're talking about."

Leo sits up. Gloria leans off her cushion and combs her orange nails into his stiff white hair. Then she presses the cool wattle under his chin.

"This show says that they didn't know, but West Nile does all kinds of things. One woman was in a wheelchair. Another guy, his whole chest was covered in these weepy sores. Jesus, I thought. Leo went to that hockey camp last summer and they don't care if kids get bit up there. Those damn things are everywhere. How can you prevent that?"

Leo is standing now. The sun scratching at his hands, his face.

"Mom…"

"They say that probably we're all gonna get it sooner or later."

Leo steps out of his nest and watches something through the window. He puts his hands on his small hips under his pyjamas.

"Mom?"

"Anyway, that's all fine and good, but we don't know what that's going to do to the population. Zebra mussels. Those little spiky fish. They say that zebra mussels clean pollution so I guess you can't say that everything's bad."

"Mom?" Leo has taken a step back from the window.

"What?" Gloria lowers the phone.

Leo suddenly squats and puts his arms up in the air.

The lower part of the window tips inward in a single piece that slides to the floor off a man's dark leg. His gloved hand punches through the upper half. He enters the room like a Slinky, feet land pulling the torso in all the way. He reaches back to a long shotgun being held out by a woman's smaller arms. He takes it from her and points it at Gloria. The blast has a concussive effect on the room, punching the TV sound away, and bouncing the dust off the floor. Gloria's left upper chest is mostly air for a second, until flesh and blood suck closed the thin tunnels pulled open by glowing shot.

The man drops the point of the gun down and he's so close to Leo that the tip sits on the crown of his head. The blast drives a blood bed downward and, yes, enough skull bone fans into brain to kill him instantly. The boy's body pops and twitches in the daylight as the gunman hands his gun back through the shattered window.

21 Pine Street

Carrots, one would have to say, are frozen and then thawed in a cycle that seems to continue forever. The sun sets and the carrot tightens, all the trees in its soft heart spider and brittle, then the sun rises and awful gases escape from the bugs buried in the carrot's head. They breathe, these short orange lungs in the pile, as they slowly and painlessly pass through the bowels of a black microbial wall.

This is part of the elaborate imaginings of Paul, an unemployed sign painter lying on the couch in his unfinished house.

The room is a tall sketch in drywall covered with boot prints and Paul watches these boot prints trailing up the wall, following each path with his eyes. His eyes do this all morning, while his mind lives, as it has for most of the month, in the compost pile he started in a bin last August. The two arenas satisfy him. The perfect collection of life and movement on the interior and the glorious bottomless hope burning in a humble plastic barrel near the sun. He starts at the top of the pile, at a six-inch stalk of broccoli. Its brown tree tops and leathery belly lie innocently, not properly part of the ground but within reach of it. A half Spanish onion becomes a gelid eye, tired and leaning further in than the broccoli. Vermicelli, its whips pooling and forming spatulate arms at rest, tired and dying, in the black heat of four avocado shells. Avocado pits, corn cobs, brown slices of bread, the molten lust of a banana splitting its purple back. Other things up here, Paul thinks, staying up for as long as he can. An eggshell; now what makes an eggshell? Ovoid. Not quite. We

love that about eggs. The shattered edge, like the face of an exploded embassy, balconies and elevator shafts held by rebars in mid-drift down to the ground. The egg is still white. Paul presses his thoughts up from the egg, out into the yard, a lone Manitoba maple; there are no eaves, just the flat black of ice and water sheathing, the drip catching edges. Unfinished roof. Paul feels a hurt in his shoulders. He has wandered to uncomfortable thoughts.

There is a boot print that seems to dominate, a long boot with a sharp and separate heel. These prints are everywhere, darker and harder than the other trails of lighter wider prints. Whenever the light ones gather, repeating themselves in the same area, the long ones circle, then intrude. Paul knows the story he watches is probably men walking, and even then, only across four-by-eight areas, which are then pulled up out of context and hung together, big flat misquotes, a puzzle solved by a monkey or an artist. John Freethy. He wore the big boots. Paul is suddenly aware of the phone, and he rolls from his back to his side in a single flip. The footprints help, at the base of the wall he now faces. They don't tell the story of these men, don't conjure names and ringing phones. Instead they look like fish. Trout as seen from a bridge. In April they run up the river by the thousands and from the bridge you can see them shuffling and hovering in the current. They are rainbow trout and when caught or when they leap they are silver and pink, but viewed from the bridge, they are grey and hollowed out by light.

Paul clips a silver-and-lime Cleo onto a leader. His head and shoulders are reflected on the water and within this some of the solid silvers come back to the fishes bodies. Paul's head is large for his small, strong body. Not quite abnormal, but differently proportioned than most people. There is a puppety look to me, he knows. It makes him presume that everyone is covering up a shameful deformity. It's a universal condition. He is an unpleasant man. He treats you like you've just said something stupid. He is vaguely aware that with each cast he's counting backwards. That's a sign he will have to go home soon.

He is already home.

The light in the room has shifted, the sun is going down. The top of the compost pile will know this, but further down, there may be no evidence of nightfall whatsoever. Here things are combined, here the microbial night is the same march of heat as the day. Heat generated by the mouths of billions of things and their bright haunches bearing down to fecalize a thick, wet, bottomless world. A world as vast and airless inside as it is across its face and even out from itself, everything, lightless and touching, a solid contiguity of inside and outside, of trace and deep heart. Purple beets are at home here. Heavy smoldering soups. Lettuce fans and frilly raspberries are now rude water and hot snot mines. A magic tinsel interior. Lungs in the chest that might as well swell up and float over our heads.

Sticky legs and pudding feet driving downward through other sticky legs and pudding feet.

Paul wants more thought like this, but it's too late to go back up. The inside has become known, its process begun. More. More. Tomato. Cucumber. Rice. Watermelon rind. A hard blue syrup on the tongues of things feeding shoulder to shoulder in a world that is completely composed of them, of these things whose eating and shitting passes through us all, a liminal hell arriving as the total insides of everything outside. A rich march of cows and wolves, who knows for sure, are they the sweep of a cape or broom? The massive eye on a single hair that bends to the ground sees it, how infinitely small is the potato, the parsley frond, the whole resistant barge of vegetable ice.

Paul gets off the couch and goes to his back yard. He wonders if there is any singing going on inside the bin. He listens. Dusk comes slowly and he has nowhere to go, nothing else to consider so he looks into this question with his new developing powers. A dog barks. Another. It's Barry Little's Blueticks. I'm outside. He puts his hands on the bin. The smell of rot moves around his face. He gives the bin a rock and the broccoli jiggles.

"Hey, Paul, your phone's disconnected."

Paul watches the carrot rapidly turn into soil then looks up.

"Oh yeah?"

It's Joseph George, the by-law officer.

"Hey, Paul, got a couple things we need to discuss."

Paul leans over the top of the bin, breathing in.

"Yeah, well. You keep me busy."

"That's good."

"I wish it was. Can we go inside?"

Paul turns and leans the small of his back against the bin. Joseph's grimacing at the smell.

"Just tell me, Joe."

Joseph sighs and pulls out a small notebook. There's a picture of a small blond boy taped to the inside cover. Paul clicks his eyelids and looks away. Payment due.

"Yeah, all your neighbours got something to say about you these days."

"Who?"

"Not important."

"Who?"

Joseph drops the notebook to his side and leans in to get closer to Paul's face.

"Everybody."

"Oh, for fuck's sake. Okay."

"Um. You can't have a broken-down car sitting on your lawn. You can't have a fridge sitting out here either. In fact, you can't have three… There another one back there?"

Joseph points to the corner of the house. Paul turns, drives his hands into his pockets.

"I got four."

"Okay. Four, that's one. Make that all one violation. Also, there's some shit against the fence, looks like tiles, big pile of it. That's gotta be disposed of. I'm gonna give you this with the codes. Let's see, what else?"

"Dogs."

"Huh? You got dogs, Paul?"

"No, but Little over there, he…"

"Okay, Paul, if you want to lodge another noise complaint against…"

"No…I think there's a criminal charge."

Joseph scratches the back of his head. The smell from the compost is harsh and sweet. He feels his stomach move near his throat.

"Okay, Paul. What?"

"You can't raise 'coon hounds."

"Oh, no?"

"No. It's illegal to hunt 'coons with hounds."

"I think he goes down to Virginia, places like that to hunt. I don't think it's illegal, Paul."

"You can't raise—"

"Paul."

"Hounds, like that, for hunting—"

"Paul."

"Fuckin' 'coons. What? What? Are you listening to me?"

Joseph puts a guiding hand behind Paul's elbow and steers him to the air conditioner sitting on a fresh concrete block at the base of the wall.

"Can we get clear of this wreck? You putting meat in that?"

"No. It's a little wet right now."

"Put leaves in it. That's what I do."

"I don't rake leaves."

"Just grab a few handfuls every once in while. Boost the carbon. You got too much nitrogen."

"Yeah, yeah…maybe. I gotta get some accelerant."

"So. What else I got? Your compost is okay. But I had four calls last week about burning."

"I was makin' hot dogs."

Paul sits on the edge of the air conditioner. Joseph rolls his eyes. It is a much-circulated fact that controlled burns are legal if they're for cooking food, so everybody sets out in the spring with a pile of leaves and branches two storeys high and a package of red hots.

"Okay. Forget the burn. There's lotsa stuff to worry about back here, Paul."

"What do you want me to say?"

"Just tell me you'll clear it out. Everything. Get that car outta here, for Christ sakes."

Paul pulls a nostril with his finger.

"Looks like a small plane crashed back here."

Joseph walks over to a small pile of bundled shingles.

"How come you haven't started finishing this place, Paul?"

Joseph steps to a window and shades his eyes as he looks in.

"This'd be a nice house."

Paul pushes himself up off the air conditioner.

"Forced air? That hooked up?"

"Nope."

Joseph presses his forehead back to the glass.

"Nope. That's your answer."

Paul can tell that his own brain is a partially eaten strawberry, and in his chest, beating rapidly, a hard bean suspended in yogurt. Knowing what's there is pointless now; the insides are all contiguous with the earth, hard and heavy and falling down.

"Okay. If this isn't done in a week, Paul, we have to think about fines."

Paul lays his head off at an angle.

"Perfect."

The sound of four car doors slamming shut in rapid succession. Near the front of the house.

Paul stands taller. Joseph looks vexed.

"You expecting somebody, Paul?"

"No. Probably nobody."

Joseph sees that Paul has no intention of announcing himself to these visitors. He wants to just stand here beside the house 'til they go away.

Glass breaking. A crashing sound. Joseph ducks then jumps up, but Paul grabs his arm.

"Shhh."

"What the hell was that?"

"Somebody's breakin' into my house, I think."

Paul feels thrilled.

"Well, come on. Let's get the police."

Paul steps quickly in Joseph's way.

"What are you doin'?"

Paul suddenly pushes Joseph up against the wall. He drives his elbow hard under Joseph's chin, causing his head to bounce hard off the brick. Paul steps back as Joseph goes down on one knee. There is blood in his hair. Paul steps back and picks up a shovel beside the compost. He raises it over his head as Joseph totters to his feet. A dark shape in the window, like Batman in an alley. Paul watches the figure. Is that a gun?

The window behind Joseph explodes and a chunk of his head flips up and down onto the lawn. Joseph takes one step forward then wallops the ground with his full body.

Paul can see now, that, yes, a man has fired a rifle into Joseph through the study window.

Paul hears himself laugh. He raises his hands.

"Okay. Okay. That's fine. I was gonna do that anyway."

A bullet touches the tip of Paul's nose, driving the skin along the underside of his brain, then out across the yard into the tree beside the compost.

23 Pine Street

The browns in here all push out, like fat men's tongues, over the edge and lay on the lip. Brown broadloom badly laid over boards and rising at the walls. Big meaty throws piled on the brown arms of a couch lying—half-hiding, really—against the sandy wall. Tom enters in from the cold, he is almost taller than the room so has to be seen from below. He presses a beetle of a cell phone into his fat chest pocket. Then he rubs his white chin with the back of his red oyster hand. A tear lands in a ladybug he imagines crawling between his knuckles. He looks for a second at the tear. It runs a crease and disappears. Big man's tear. Big man crying. Tom holds his chin as he cries. He pushes back on his teeth whenever emotion bucks them forward. He puts out his other hand to feel where he'll sit if he has to. A car door. Tom breathes with his mouth wide open, then holds the air in.

The door behind him opens with a shake. Tom releases the breath through his nose, trying to reclaim his chest from involuntary movement and the pig-like racket of crying.

Hedy is standing on the mat behind him.

"Wipers are acting up."

She kicks the bottom stair to knock snow off her soft black boots. She looks at her husband's back. Man's big as a field.

"Did you hear what I said?"

Tom moves forward into the room turning his head to his shoulder. He's too big to pretend to be doing anything.

"Need winter wipers. I told you."

Hedy lays her soft gloves on the radiator.

"Yeah, well."

Tom and Hedy's son's wife went missing ten days ago. She had been canoeing in the lake and never returned. She is presumed dead. Tom fishes for rainbow trout from the shore in the fall and spring. He fears two things. That he will hook her body one day. That he will eat a fish that ate her. He loved her very much. Her voice made him happy.

She wears a long coat of red suckers. Long and living backs up and down her body.

"You okay?"

Tom sits down on the couch. "No. I don't think I…" A part of his lung breaks like a girl. He puts his hands to his face. Red cheeks billow like elephant ears.

The heavy jig pulls the roe bag down from the light. Past a pale canopy of tiny orange ferns and suspended silt, the dark hook drives to the bottom. Her arm is green and red. In a smooth sac of ice. The hook disappears in her hair. She will be brought home this way, pulled by a rusted point stuck in her crown.

Hedy sighs and touches his heavy coat on the shoulder.

"You want a coffee?"

"No."

"You didn't act like this when your sister died."

Hedy stares for a moment. He is motionless. He has stopped crying and just sits there. Enormous hands on monster knees. He thinks that she thinks that in him there is a useless sadness. He raises the end of his scarf off his arm and turns it in the air so it comes off the back of his neck.

"Okay. Well. She's dead. I don't need to say anything about that today."

The light is fading in the long window over the couch. It looks like nightfall, but it's only one o'clock in the afternoon. A false night. A streamer coming off the bay.

"Don't look at me. I don't like anybody to die."

Tom bangs the side of his nose with his thumb and watches his wife. She pulls a small box off the top of a shelf. She pushes a button on a CD player. The music of Clay Aiken. She sits in her own chair and opens the small box and pulls out a miniature silver Rolls Royce. She carefully slips a neatly folded piece of paper from beneath the molded felt bed that held the car.

Tom leans to one side and pulls out his left arm, then repeats this action for the right. He lifts a TV remote from an iron sleigh sitting on the glass table.

"Can we turn that shit off?"

Hedy looks over the tops of her glasses at him. Big crying Tom. Shameless man. We can't all be carefree dead girls. She touches something at her side and the music stops.

She returns to the piece of paper. It is folded into sixteenths and when open is a cubelike cootie catcher, a page of dents.

On the TV, the weather. The squalls are set up for the afternoon and will continue into the evening, giving local accumulations of up to thirty centimetres.

The piece of paper is a certificate of authenticity. The Rolls Royce is a limited edition replica made of silver plate by the artisan Geoffrey Haterfiledes.

"They said it was gonna be sunny. They don't know nothing."

Tom changes the channel. A bass fishing derby. The fish doesn't want to get weighed.

Hedy looks up. "Getting paid to fish. That's not a job. How do you pronounce this H-A-T-E-R-F-I-L-E-D-E-S?"

Tom looks over as he changes the channel.

He looks at this woman who studies the provenance of a ten-dollar piece of junk but can't credit a meteorologist.

The window smashes and Tom hunches forward. Hedy drops the Rolls. Glass falls in pie pieces, landing and turning off the sill. A rude looking rock sits on the carpet.

"What the fuckin'…?"

The door is kicked in.

"What the hell's going on?"

The man steps forward and swings a fireman's axe down. It hits Tom on the shoulder, driving his body deep in the chair. He draws the handle down hard and Tom's heaviness unfolds across the floor.

Hedy looks on. Clearly this is the first time in her life that something big is happening that absolutely cannot be happening. The axe head comes up and she sees the red meat of her husband. Tom bellows and pushes himself onto his back. The man brings the axe down again, this time hitting Tom square on the face with the blunt end. Hedy watches as the left side of her husband's face presses against the right's side then disappears under the dense gore of an iron head.

She feels panic flipping into her hair then leaving. Everything is slowed down by cliché.

The axe head has one third of the contents of her husband's left eye swinging off a corner. This third is merely fluid and a small section of the eye bag itself. The pupil and nerve stem are in the dark hole of his head. When the axe head reaches an apex it stops completely. It will be turned so that the blade faces Hedy in the chair. While it is stopped Hedy looks at the man. His face is straining in the effort to change the direction he is swinging the axe. No other expression, just strain.

Inside he's saying, "I have to get this axe turned around so that the blade goes into that lady." He's not saying anything else to himself.

Hedy watches the axe completely turn. The edge of the blade looks like a closed eye that suddenly opens and flashes down. It hits on the corner of her head, breaking her skull before falling down like a cow to its knees onto her shoulder, crashing through and exploding the side of her heart. Hedy is still looking, still seeing, though she will die in a moment or two.

Tom is hanging on a bit longer. Surprising because some of his teeth are imbedded in his spinal cord.

The girl is floating like a red candy moon in a pink milk sky. She is stiff and cold and covered with a soft film. The stars watch her. The lake is calm and black. Soon the ice will harden again and she will stop. If we could stand on her we could see the fires burning in Collingwood.

28 Pine Street

Around the room on sills and rims and hoops and borders stand the millions of things and, here, selectively, are some of them: Little blue men with umbrellas, a dog facing Jesus, a bracelet on ceramic bonsai, four slender race cars sharing a bean, a yellow park bench the size of a mouse, paper doilies, yellow shag carpet specked with tiny blue dots slung over a radiator. The TV looks like an airport gypsy leaning against a locker. It winks and flashes a single gold tooth; there are several game shows rolled into one. The couch is buried under filthy throws beneath a painting of a wolf crying under a watery moonscape. Rose's fat white feet are up off the floor. She holds a small dirty dog against her warm front. A bird on her shoulder punches her big ear with its face. Smaller and more like the other things in the room is Mike. He appears to be a smoke-damaged doll, brown and sore and thin. He rocks slightly, occasionally giving the TV his assent: "Yep. Yep. Yep."

"Well, I think you should just smoke. My dad smoked and he was ninety-two when he died."

Mike looks over, stricken deeply by these remarks, though as he blinks, near tears, they are still seconds from being understood.

"Smoke. Smoke."

Mike shrugs, knowing now that it's better to dismiss this.

"Chelsea, there's glue on them."

A little girl, Chelsea, sits on the floor and links tiny tires in her long red hair. She drops her pale hands from her hair. Sticky black tires hang in orange leopard spots. She tips her head to feel the tires touch her cheeks.

"Don't listen, then." Rose reaches up to her shoulder and bumps her hand against the bird's back. "Why did he prescribe you an anti-depressant?"

Mike's hands jump from oddly effeminate poses around his face to the arms on his chair.

"Junior's not good. He told me to give her Dimetapp. That's not gonna help allergies."

A sharp cry from the floor. Chelsea holds up a plastic tire tangled in her hair.

"You should go to the emerge on Sundays, when Green's there."

Mike agrees suddenly with his right hand, then disagrees abruptly with his mouth. Rose stares at him for a moment.

"I can't believe gambling is a side effect."

Mike affirms this with a bristled chin scratching into his shoulder.

Rose tilts on her round thighs and delicately delivers the bird from the back of her fat hand through the open door of a tall white cage.

"Gary Taylor's eldest girl was given the same as you for compulsive spending. How can one pill stop a teenager from buyin' clothes and then send a alcoholic to the casino like a madman?"

The phone rings. Rose clips the cage door closed before scooping up the phone.

"Hello."

She takes small pride in what she does next. She grunts and hangs up. Rose likes it when her world knows her so well that she doesn't have to use a lot of words, even though does, and will, because it's awful quiet around here sometimes.

"Yer mom's here."

Chelsea is trying to hang tires in front of her eyes. She tilts her head back and regards the door haughtily.

The door opens and a stocky woman with yellow hair enters.

"It's awful quiet out there."

Mike sits up and tries to look past the woman. Rose pulls her ankles further under her rear.

"Mike spent eighty dollars on Nevada."

Chelsea's mom has dark eyes, pretty but hard. She laughs, then looks at her daughter. "What's this one doin'?"

"I told her to get them outta her hair. She'll like it when I hafta pull 'em out."

Gretch reaches down and draws Chelsea up to stand.

"You have such pretty hair. Why you wanna do that?"

Chelsea lowers her eyes and pretends to sob. Mike, Rose and Gretch stare at her, until Gretch turns away and points out the window.

"There's nobody around out there."

"So you say."

"It's weird."

A small *tick* sound as a hole appears in the glass. Rose and Gretch look at the hole and lean up to look into the yard.

Mike stares straight ahead. At the same moment as the *tick* sound, a bullet entered Chelsea's forehead and she has dropped dead in the middle of the floor. Mike makes a horrible low gurgle. Gretch turns to say something and sees her daughter folded over on the carpet.

Rose screams.

25 Pine Street

The bedroom is a girl's. Dora the Explorer with her massive head
and eyes the size of pies hangs by a loop off the edge of a mirror. A
pony with a cream-coloured saddle, blue diapers made out of sky, a
ladle stolen from a cardboard box, a plastic house. A little grey space
heater sits three feet from the side of her bed. An egg glowing in a
goalie's mask. She should have been asleep hours ago, but she is
scared. Not of the dark, not of a monster, not about whether
mommy and daddy can stay friends. No, what little Heather, with
her funny pale face framed by red, red ringlets is scared of is Osama
Ben Lawdy. His name keeps coming up, in whispered ways
sometimes. In caves near Ravenna.

Heather hears her parents yelling below, then gunshots. She
listens and hears nothing. The front door slams. It *was* Osama Ben
Lawdy and now he's gone.

Heather finally sleeps.

18 Pine Street

Ed is lying on his side. Near his thigh a bag of chips, under his head a thick pillow. He drags chip crumb knuckles through his chest, laying hairs down with light oil.

The television he watches is in a stand-up Pac-Man game console. On the screen is a B4-4 video. Beside it a teddy bear-themed pinball machine. Ed's phone number is displayed where the high score should be. A vintage black rotary dial phone on the floor. It rings.

Ed crushes chips under his steamroller thigh to reach the phone.

"Hello?"

"Hi. It's me."

Me is Glenda. She's calling from Sault Ste. Marie. She met Ed on the internet three weeks ago.

"Oh, hi."

"Hi."

"…"

"What's wrong?"

"Nothin'."

"…"

"Are you busy?"

"No."

"Are you mad?"

"No."

"Then what?"

The B4-4 video ends with a surprising reveal that the video "chick" is a lesbian. Ed tries to imagine what this means to people younger than him.

"Are you there?"

"Yeah. I'm here."

"I'll talk to you later."

"Okay."

"..."

"..."

"Are you in a bad mood?"

Ed sighs and rubs the prickles on his cheek.

"You're in a bad mood a lot."

Ed makes a sound into the phone, nearly an explaining sound.

"I just found out that my old landlord wants me to pay for the carpet he says I ruined."

"Oh."

"I don't care. I just won't answer the phone for a while."

Finally another video. Mariah Carey. Ed writes her name down on a piece of paper. He runs a karaoke business called Waygooze Productions and he has a gig with a benefit for the Stayner Skateboard Park. He can't figure out whether to get music for kids or adults. Sometimes they listen to the same things.

A bullet hits Ed in the elbow and he flinches. Glenda hears his breath go in but not come out.

"So. My family says I should just tell you where to go."

Ed sees red rushing up from an underground well in his arm. A second bullet enters his chest, making a temporary cone out of his heart.

"I defend you, you know."

57 Pine Street

Bob Venton's head is bobbing and his green Bing Crosby hat goes down down like wet wax on a candle. This little alcove at the side of the Tim Hortons is the wing of a stage. Bob has recently tried to lay claim to the name "Jazz in the Park" so that he could sell it to Meaford. He did run the Jazz in the Park in Wasaga Beach, a blaring festival of John Williams movie soundtracks that scared the walleye from the edges of Nancy Island, but he doesn't own the title. Wasaga Beach is looking for him. He has spent the winter running a Cole Porter review in the basement of The River Inn. Tickets were twenty-five dollars a pop, and shows ran nightly through the winter months. He expected to get twenty to thirty people a night so he could bankroll his musical about the Collingwood shipyards. He has already written the opening number about shipbuilders spending their money on hookers. Unfortunately, only thirteen people showed up to see *Baby, It's Cole Outside*. Thirteen people. All winter. Now Bob Venton's on the run. It's hard to say exactly from what. Unpaid musicians or yet another municipal grift involving parks and rec. He stands here, hat dropping to hand and plans to enter the Tim Hortons in order to borrow money so he can buy a coffee. People'll think he left his wallet somewhere. Money just out of reach. A nickel on a bird's head or a dime popped up off a tin can. Bobby's eyes, so close together that they make each other nervous, speaks through a little rubber beak. He speaks in a kind of scat.

"Hey, big daddies. Man, that's a day to be big."

Bobby rubs his ear, as if to erase what he's just said. Barry Little looks up, his big owl face reddening.

"Hi, Bobby. What can I do for you?"

"Ah. Be-dap. Be doo. Man, I just need some…to boot me some geets."

Barry sighs and draws coffee from the edge of his cup.

"Mash me a fin, pops?"

"Not readin' ya, Sammy Davis."

Other patrons are trying to hide behind steam.

Bobby snaps his fingers. "Sorry, daddy-o. My jib is on a slide."

Barry blinks froggishly.

"Sorry, mack. My jive is off-time and—"

"Shut up, Bobby…"

"Hey, pops. Hey, daddy. Hey—"

"Bobby."

"But…"

"Bobby."

Bobby pauses, pointing his index fingers out and down. His expression is very sad. "Could ya see me for a cup of Joe, Barry?"

Barry shifts his heavy left hip up as he forages through a pocket. Bobby rocks his fingers back and forth, shooting imaginary guns off into the floor.

"Fly me to the moon. Hey."

When Barry holds out the coins, Bobby sweeps his hat out under his hand. Barry is embarrassed by this and looks up at Bobby. Bobby's hair has formed into a greasy fin under the hat. His eyes so very close together. Barry releases the coins into the hat. Bobby winks and clicks his tongue.

Bobby stands behind a thin mechanic in dirty overalls. Bobby is almost too nervous to wait for his coffee. He begins tapping his feet, shuffling his heels.

"When the shark bites. Yeah. With his teeth, man."

The mechanic turns slowly and fixes a look on Bobby, stopping him suddenly. Never at a complete loss, Bobby extends his arm and pops his hat into the air toward his head. A quarter hits him in the eye and he doubles over. Some dimes and nickels tinkle to the floor as Bobby holds his eye. He stomps on the coins to stop their spinning.

"Bobby?"

Bobby has one hand over his eye. It's the manager of Tim Hortons. A tight-skinned man with hard black hair.

"Did you hurt yourself there?"

"No, man. No."

"Okay. Look, you're gonna have to leave."

Bobby stops for a moment, as if to give him the chance to take that back.

"You can't be...uh...borrowing money here."

Bobby smiles and puts his hat on. His eye is blood red. A final quarter slips from the inner brim and sticks to the sweat on his forehead.

"Okay. I'm sorry, man. I'm sorry."

"It's okay, Bobby. No, I'm sorry...look, it's just I can't..."

"I'll just go."

Bobby's eyes wobble like a compass to find each patron, then settle on an empty table.

The sun is powe.ful outside and Bobby has to cover his injured eye. Before he steps off the curb, the manager comes out with a coffee, nods, says nothing and slips back in.

To get to Meaford from Stayner you have to take Highway 26 through downtown Collingwood and along the base of Blue Mountain to Thornbury and finally, the tiny, pretty harbour town of Meaford pops up. Bobby's hitchhiking inland, to Duntroon, then back out to Collingwood.

The fields between Duntroon and Stayner lie like drapery across a foot, curling and swooping in fine detail, lazily folded backwards or cinched by a stand of crabapple trees. This is the valley Bobby walks in. Crows as big as cows pull at meat near the road's edge. Poles lift the lines up, up and onto Duntroon's distant brown puff. It is rural paperwork country. Quarries pull the white from the grey ground and long tree farms sit in paragraghs. Bobby walks into his valley like a man in search of a blue bird. Whistling, his one good eye scanning the pale escarpment, Bobby realizes at the pit of the valley that he hadn't planned on walking up the other side. He throws out his thumb.

A pickup truck descends from behind, from where Duntroon tips over onto the mountain, and it races down pulling a hell-wig of dust. The driver sees in the distance poor Bobby Venton, his big feet pigeon stepping, his hands thrust in pockets as if to keep luck from flying out of them. His crooner's hat, with its crushed felt and tiny red feather, mark him as a man who walks at the bottom of a giant screen, a movie bearing down on him, swinging like a dream into the valley.

In the back of the pickup are four boys from Ravenna. They are heading to Stayner to raid the co-op for axes. The killers have been shooting their guns too liberally and have run out of rounds. The job will have to be finished with farm implements.

Bobby turns at the sound of the truck. He watches as it crosses the median. Bobby steps back onto the shoulder, but not fast enough. The truck clips his hip, sending him twirling in the air like a baton, up and over the fence, headfirst into an immature field of corn.

The driver looks in his rearview. The road is empty and his boys are quiet.

Bobby lies still on his side, bent at the waist like a safety pin. His lower spine and hip are shattered, but he is still breathing.

We look to heaven and send up our thanks for this small life spared. A life barely worth living in a body that, though lying still, is heading violently in two directions at once. He will come to, then die.

35 Main Street

Murray is on the second landing of the fire stairs going up the clock tower. There are no windows, but people are going up and down these stairs all the time and he asks them about what's happening. He was wounded last Friday. He had come to Main Street from Pine. He was going to get a coffee when two children with pitchforks jumped out of the back of a van and lunged at him. One of the forks went into his knee and the other into his ribs. They had him like this, trying to pull his leg off and push his heart out. A man came from somewhere and he struck one of the kids in the face with a bat. It was a real fast swing that curled the kid back and dead before he hit the ground. Murray saw one of the kid's eyes on the lawn. The other kid dropped his pitchfork, or rather, left it in Murray and ran. God knows where.

Murray saw bits of things. It was a nice day. The sun was shining, and it was hot, but Collingwood has all this shade on its sidewalks so, rather than oppressed, you feel pampered. But this was crazy. The man with the bat asked Murray something that Murray couldn't make out. He was terrified. He seemed to know what Murray didn't at this point. The people of Ravenna had gone nuts. They had invaded Collingwood over night. They were trying to kill Collingwood. The man managed to get the pitchfork from Murray's ribs, but before he could free his leg, something scared him off. He ran up over his front lawn and down the side of his house. The holes in Murray's chest didn't feel deep, not mortally deep, but he had this fork fully driven through his leg above the knee. The man with the bat had completely abandoned Murray to the sidewalk. The child on the grass was dead. The sky so clear. Why was this happening? Murray tried to pull the pitchfork out, but it was angled down. He just couldn't move well enough to get a hold of it. He didn't want to cry out for help because he was so uncertain about what was happening. Time passed. The clouds were lengthening, like white canoes drooping down over town. What was all this? Murray began to fear that there had been some kind of evacuation or something. He couldn't hear cars or people or anything. But in Collingwood? Why would people invade Collingwood? Those kids had jumped out of a van. Someone had been helping them. The driver had seen him walking along and slowed down, stopped and sent those kids out to kill. The van had pulled away again, he thought. When that man killed the boy. Murray's chest has stopped bleeding. There are three black clots on his shirt. His leg, though, it's still bleeding. Not pouring, but oozing. He can't be completely still, because of the weight of the pitchfork. He feels like a piece of food sitting on a plate.

"Help!"

He has to. He has to cry out. He didn't even know why he was being quiet.

"Help!"

He hears a door open at the house where the man disappeared. A woman's voice.

"No! No!"

Then the man:

"I have to tell him what to do."

Murray thinks this is crazy. He calls out:

"Do what? What do I have to do?"

A shadow closes the sun. The man stage whispers:

"Can you walk?"

"No. Not with this in my leg. Help me."

He puts his hand hard onto Murray's leg then hauls on the pitchfork. Murray whines as it slides out. Murray sees the blood rising up and spilling out. The man pushes his hand on the holes. Murray screams and the hand darts away.

"No. No. You have to be quiet. Okay. C'mon."

An arm slides under Murray. The woman's voice from afar:

"Leave him. There's a truck coming. Leave him."

Murray is dropped.

"Pretend you're dead. Sorry."

He's gone and now Murray can hear the truck. It's coming down Pine Street towards Hurontario. Why does he have to pretend to be dead?

The truck stops beside Murray and he lies still. He's lying on the sidewalk pretending to be dead.

Do I close my eyes? he thinks. He doesn't even know how to act dead. He finds a cloud and stares at it, however it's moving quickly and he's aware of his eyes drifting upward. He locks them open and blank. Dead. Pretend dead.

He hears the truck door open and moments later it slams closed. The truck idles noisily. Two men talk. He can see the blur of them at the periphery of his dead vision.

"He's breathing."

He stops breathing. His eyes sting.

A face closes in on him. A wrinkled face. A little scar on his chin. Bright grey bristles.

"Are you playin' dead?"

He's doing what he was told to do.

"I'll tell ya."

He has a wobbly orange ball in front of him, filling the sky. He thinks his eyes are burning out.

A shape cuts into the ball. He smells gas. His lips open and gas flows between them. The orange balls explodes in his lungs and he rolls over but pain has arrived in his leg now. "Jesus!"

"He killed this boy. Kill him."

He presses his face to the sidewalk and is surprised when he falls asleep.

He can't recall being asleep like this ever before in his life. He has left the situation, but is still aware that things are very dangerous. He tries to feel his way back. If I'm being killed now, he thinks, I want to know. He pays close attention to how he feels. If I am unconscious, he thinks, how will I know when I shift from being asleep to being dead? Where are my hands? He thinks they are flopping upward. Either limply as his body is being transported, or weakly because he's still trying to protect himself. He can't tell. Limply, weakly. Then they get solid again. He drives his elbow up to knock them away, but they are not there. He stands up and looks at the empty street. No blood. No boy. No pitchfork. Had he imagined all of that? Had it happened?

What is it with this war? The fighting goes on and every day that passes gets us further and further from the day before it all started. The things that were normal. The Fernwood Farms corn maze on Airport Road. The used car lot in a cow field on Fairgrounds Road. The ancient barn on the Poplar Sideroad, so overgrown by vines that it looks like a giant green oven in the middle of a flat field. Things you see and say to your friends. "Well, it's nice. A little out of the ordinary." And nobody disagrees. My God, this is a place where nobody disagrees. If someone, the mother of the woman who owns the barber shop, say, does disagree, she says, "I don't think they should breed coon hounds in town." But, you know, Barry Little breeds coon hounds at the edge of town. Does he still fall under some by-law code against breeding? Yes. Yes, he certainly does. But we all understand that he's at the edge, and if we can't come to agree that people who are at the edge can't do a little more than us at the middle, then we have become ruled by the rules. We bend a little. She was not bending. She wants to catch us all. This big woman with a face like a tire, she can just go fuck herself today.

"Hey, Mr. Man."

Murray puts his gloves on a *Maclean's* magazine.

"How are ya?"

"Well, we're just fine, I bet." He smiles and sits beside Barry Little. In the mirror.

Annie is the barber. She's got a face like the sun, only made out of margarine. Ugly, sunny woman. "You need a haircut, Mister."

Murray rolls his eyes around. She treats all the men like children. Barry Little rubs his nose and gives Murray a look.

The door opens and a small man enters. "Hey, Annie." He nods to Murray and for some reason ignores Barry. "Hey, Annie, does your mom have cancer?"

Annie pauses, adjusts her scissors in the air over the boy's head.

"'Cause two people now have told me she's got cancer and lost all this weight and I figured I'd just come ask you."

"Mom!" Annie calls, continues cutting, ignoring everyone.

"Hey. You don't have to call her. You can tell me. Jesus."

Annie's mother is bigger than Annie and is built like a government dock. "What? Oh, it's busy. Hi, Barry. You wanna hand, Annie?"

"Sure, mom. Hey, Mr. Jonstad here is asking after your health."

Mom looks at Mr. Jonstad. "It's fine."

Mr. Jonstad is embarrassed.

"Did you want a haircut?"

Mr. Jonstad mumbles no. Apologizing, he backs out of the store.

Mom slings a thin apron across her watery middle. "Everybody thinks I got the cancer. I don't have the damn cancer and if I did it would be my business."

Annie is cutting air around the boy's head. Trimming a halo she can see. Mom signals to me.

"I think Barry's first."

Barry speaks finally. "Oh. You go first. You get your haircut first."

All the time Mom's cutting my hair I can see Barry's face.

"Hey, Barry. How's the Blueticks?"

He looks up. "Did you complain about my dogs to George?"

"Joseph George?"

"Yeah. By-law."

"Nope."

Barry slaps his knee and grabs his chin. His face is bright red.

"You bet somebody did. And I want a last name and a first name off somebody."

When these people die, that is, now, there is so much glass breaking and screaming. The shot from five guns enters the front window at the same moment. It is enough for now to say that they are dead. The street is long and many, many more will die in the minutes ahead.

The Clock Tower

They were on the second floor, four of them, Clarence, two teens
and a hockey mom. None of them had slept in forty-eight hours and
they had gone through their last Timbits hours ago. Mom had
dragged a plastic suitcase of cordless powertools up the stairs and
now she sits with saws—Skil and reciprocating. One of the teenage
boys has a pitchfork and the other has a baseball bat. Clarence has a
javelin that he took from the high school. They are in strategic
positions. There are two doors that open to this landing. Pitchfork
boy sits by one and baseball bat by the other. When someone comes
through a door, one of the boys brings him down by either driving
the pitchfork or swinging the bat. The enemy goes down or at least
stumbles and Clarence hurls the javelin at their torso. Then Mom
descends with her blade spinning. She goes for the neck, pushing the
blade as hard as she can, opening up a lethal wound. Her job is
important because a man down with a broken leg and a hole in his
gut can absolutely get back up, so when Mom opens the throat, he
gives up. They want him to know right away that he is dying and
then to lie down and do it. It takes time. The dying lie there spilling
and gurgling until they stop.

They know that there is one guy left up in the tower top. They
have two of his buddies rolled against the wall. Below them there
could be hundreds. As long as he's up there signaling his situation,
enemy is gonna try to get up here. They have to make a move.

"He has a shotgun."

Mom is pulling skin out from behind her blade. The blade only spins about fifteen seconds before it gets jammed. She manages to get through an artery or two in the throat before it clogs. The wound has to feel like a tap or the enemy keeps coming. If it isn't quite there the boys hold him down while she pushes the Sawzall through the throat and right into the chest cavity. She snaps what looks like a red rubber band from the saw's spindle, sets it down and looks at Clarence.

"Yes, he has a shotgun. And we don't know where he is, do we?"

"He's probably looking out on the street. Got his back to the door."

"I dunno. That door's more dangerous to him. He's waiting for us."

Clarence climbs out of his crossed legs and steps over to the door. He puts an ear to it. The blood on the floor has pooled under the door. "He sees this," he says, tapping the blood with his boot.

Pitchfork lifts his pitchfork. "Yeah, he knows we wanna get him."

"So how do we?"

Mom has a battery charger and she grunts as she switches batteries on the floor. "We're like a cat. These boys are the paws knockin him down, you're the claws keeping him down and I'm the teeth that finish him off. We just gotta get through the door and do it all at once."

"Cats explode."

Baseball bat nods to pitchfork.

"We gotta get through that door and explode."

"Kick the door in and the boys go low. As they pounce across the floor swingin' and stabbin', Mom, you leap high through the door. You'll be dashing behind him and he'll have to swerve 'cause you'll look like the biggest threat. Then as the boys crack at his feet and he's wheelin' that big old gun back down, I jump in straight and go right in the chest. You boys don't stay there. You roll away fast, get behind him and pull him down. If you can. I'll jump at the gun and try and get it while Mom, you come in and cut him real deep and fast. Hopefully I'll have the gun by then and you boys just put everything at his head. Smash that head right in."

Mom and the boys look at each other and squint.

"Has to be real fast."

"We gotta explode."

"Like a cat."

"That's right. A cat."

"Okay."

Clarence steps back from the door and places a hand on Mom's shoulder as she drives a battery pack into the end of the Sawzall, then the Skil. She looks up at him without meeting his eyes. Her mouth pulls down in readiness. She crouches in front. The boys shimmy on their knees to the sides of the door. They hold their weapons in two hands. They look back at Clarence and he shakes his head once quickly to empty his expression. He takes two fast strides and lands a foot sideways. The door stays and he goes down. Biting pain in his hip. He lifts both legs to kick from where he lies and a hole explodes in the middle of the door. He kicks and the door goes in, sucking smoke over him. He sees the boys tumble across his legs and before he can roll to stand, Mom leaps diagonally through the air.

Up. Up. His thighs crunch painfully. A blast. The room is brighter than Clarence thought it would be and he sees only swirls for a moment. Then a man in a suit pitching forward. Clarence hurls the javelin and it just catches the man's back. It looks like a hook in a fly as the man flails to the side, wriggling against his superficial but painful wounds.

The saw whines, then stops. There is someone else here. Mom is pulling the Skil off the throat of a young woman. Clarence hears the telltale sound. The woman falls from Mom's knees and begins

her death leak. The boys are whacking at the man's head; the bat
busts his hand open and the pitchfork enters his forehead. He's gone.

Clarence sweeps down and gets the shotgun. The tower window
is broken. He goes to it and leans the gun up, lowers it and watches
the street. A group of heavy men burst out of the donut shop and
make for the entrance. He shoots down, opening a tunnel on a man's
head. The boys heave the dying man and woman out the window
and they fall to the sidewalk below. The sidewalk is empty. The
enemy is on its way up.

They retreat to the room. Mom is touching her shoulder. The
shotgun has taken a bite out of her. She says "Oh . . ." softly. Clarence
hears footsteps as the boys close the door. The door is destroyed.
They look around for something to block the way.

"Fuck it. Get on the sides."

The boys stand on either side of the door. Mom has fainted or something. She's down anyway. No help.

The first guy comes through. He looks at Clarence. He's surprised. The boys have busted his shins right out of the flesh. He goes down and then there are two more. One falls over the first and Clarence poles him in the back of the skull. The other manages to fire something before the kids whip his teeth down his throat. Clarence got a bullet or something under his ribs and can feel his whole left side turning to water. He goes down, but manages to pry a gun out of somebody's hand. He fires and gets a chubby boy's throat to come out. The boys watch him aim. There's a pile of bodies accumulating and now there's big guys flying into the room. The kids' sticks are breaking in the air. These big boys won't be swatted down. They go for the kids, two on each, and hammer them very hard. The men straighten up and look around. They step over Clarence to the watchtower window. I must look dead or something, Clarence thinks. His eyes are open, though, so he's a little confused. One man calls down that everyone is dead now. That means Clarence. They leave.

Clarence can see Mom's hands to his left. Looks like they finished her off. The kids, too. They're broken to pieces over there. He does hear someone groaning. A lean guy. Bald. He sits up, breathing hard. He has a bright pink hole in his cheek that he pats at, then winces.

He stares at Clarence for a while. There is an explosion below. The floor curls around Clarence's legs, then pulls taut again.

The winter will be very long.

The Entertainment District

Someone stood on my hand in the night. They mustn't have seen me. Which is good. They might have thought I was a heavy bag or a rolled up carpet. I don't go out of my way to hide myself in the day, but I do look for places out of the sun. Sunken stairwells I like. Recesses. Spots that are not open. Wind goes elsewhere if your walls are all touching you. But last night someone found me. Didn't find me, actually. Stepped on me. My hand. Pressure on the fingers, splaying them as I slept. Dreamed of being stepped on. So now that night has fallen I am going to move. I lift and leap to the roof of a shed in the alley then I drop to the narrow curb running against the grass here. I can move silently and rapidly on things that are four inches wide. My feet can grab and release the ground fast when they know what to expect. Up at fire escape. One arm and hand over and I am up four flights in three moves, then using the momentum up to the flat roof. I don't stop but move. The pebbly surface means I run instead of jump, but still a blur then I'm on the front, four floors up. I don't look to see who's in there. A man is standing by the entrance to a hallway. I push off the wall with my feet and move clean through his back with the balled fist. His spine hits the floor like dice and then a woman in purple. She is going to turn but I draw one of her arms off and keep going. The blood is loud as it lands. Kitchen empty, I think. Then gone. The apartment hall is great. Both feet halfway up opposing walls and knees don't even have to pump. Just the spring at the ankle and I'm like water in a hose. Stairwell down,

but I don't remember. Then the street, which I hate, one older man
is just a momentary wetness on my chest and left arm then two
teenage girls sort of pop like bubbles and leave a young red wind
underfoot. Then the recycle box and halfway up a light standard onto
the side of a building above pizza. A man in the window. Can't not,
so I make the glass tiny and stop by him for a moment. Don't know
if he sees, but I get one hand on his jaw and the other on top and turn
it upwards. I remove the centre and see the door loose so go. I drop
some of the middle of his head and because I'm in a hurry it gets
bent around the door frame before something else happens to it.
Didn't notice the dog so I take one step back and one forward to

drive the chest apart. Feel a little like I'm wasting my time with things that don't matter. Three at the elevator who saw the dog go down and don't see me come around off the corner and because three together is not going to happen again for almost a minute I watch where I put things. His hands up into her back and out pointing down into the other's eyes. The fingers are hard and sharp at this speed so they scoop in and are bested by the back of the skull. Hard to know exactly how that ends, but I get a little spasm in my own finger. Could be anything. Probably pass. Gone already. The street again feels like I've been here all night and so onto a streetcar two steps, then a car, foot goes through and feel somebody up around it. Light suction as I get out. Red light. Jump to orange. And a hall. Big hall. Music. Land on the third floor but keep going. Don't know what but this is just the way it has to go. Hard to say and do at the same time. Two shoulders. Use somebody's hand to stand and it goes out. Chest and three run. I think there is a sense that I am here. Decide to try a slap and four vertebra go under a scalp so worth again and this time the whole shoulder comes off and for a moment looks like you could cook it. Unexpected that it's its own side event and have to look back to see. It turns an old woman's stomach into its cloth. He yelling so I do my feet in a quick circle to take out just eyes. Only eyes with tips of feet. Feel good and use the circle as a way of going straight up. You never go straight up and I smear a caged light on the wall. Make it up far enough to reach a beam and dive waiting for my feet to grab and that is a very very advantageous way to pull so the beam comes free at the end I left and I have enough going that I can just hold on as I go through the concrete wall. The beam falls but I am going so fast that I have no idea. Dark, which I like, and people, probably thousands under. The move is amazing. I go probably six hundred feet without having to do anything. I should though and I hit the far side hard and fall. Don't like falling and it makes me mad. And slow. I make a mess. I pull a throat clear out and onto somebody so bad that the throat is part of his head before he dies. Then, still mad, I push a girl into what might be her boyfriend and her arm is bagged by his left lung. Keep going 'cause I'm stuck until I feel better. I punch, which I rarely do, and face caves like bubble wrap. Try this: put two shoulders into each other so pressure makes the stomach fizz out between the legs. Slap, slap, slap…eyes and teeth in a braid, then a tongue as if it's happy to be doing this, goes forever. I feel

stupid. Like a bomb, so I move. Just feet to floor but I pump hard and feel people slip over me like hot food. Hold the last person at the door and under me they are a temporary sled. I lie on this wet person and go down the hall. The ground comes up through them pretty quick so I tap the friction quick and that sends me up through a tall window above the main entrance. Streetcar. I go too far and, luckily, into an alley and some papers there and a red light and another fire escape at the end which I bend going up, as turns out, twenty-three storeys. My steam takes me a few dozen more feet into open air then down. Gravity, in spite of what you may think, slows me down. I am pushing against a second force that is terrible lazy and stubborn. I swing in at the fifteenth floor and divide a dog, a man, and three children into 3,989,793 pieces, each one is cone-shaped for one very impressive second then recombines as muck. I check my watch and realize I need to be somewhere.

Rural Route #4

The face is what Joseph expects. Roman numerals on the hour marker and a complete non-numerated minute track. It is framed in a hinged brass bezel that sits snugly in a wood bezel. Beneath this he sees less. The pendulum assembly with its brass manta, stops, and springs. He is aware of the mighty and gold lenticular bob as it is, a genital to say and a genital to watch. The case has a side inspection door and at the bottom, behind the bob, a hatch. The key is there too, the winding and the bottom door key, which are often missing from these old mechanicals. It has been wound and the time is correct though who knows how she keeps it. It's easy enough to bend over when the attention's elsewhere and push a hand. He doesn't know if it's working, and this upsets him unreasonably. He could ask, but he will be told either that it works perfectly or that it is as it is. Its gong could have an ugly sound and no matter where you mount it you will hear this. It might need winding constantly and slip when you try. It may be something he will neglect. Regret. Sitting on the wall like a shadow. It might be a last straw of some kind. He might be acquiring his last straw and not even know it. But if it is that, a last straw, isn't it the best of all the straws? Isn't the last straw the one that makes an impossible burden finally what it should be? Does he get this thing, which he'll call fine, because he knows, or hopes that it's not? He looks twelve or so inches past that to a shallow sheet metal case. Homemade. The green surface paint is chipped and scratched. Rust orange and two circular black marks and a heavy diagonal

smear that may be a burn scar. The clasp on the side is loose. He flips the lid. Four or five screwdrivers. Each from a different set. Translucent handles. Green. Red. The Phillips has a messy, burred tip. There's an old slip of wood. A level. He closes the case lightly, more lightly than anyone has in years. An ashtray with a clear glass plate circled by a heavy rubber replica of a snow tire. Ten hacksaw blades. An old Palm Pilot. It looks big as a box spring. The stylus missing. There are pick axes under the table. None of this stuff, at least nothing at this table, is going to help him. He pushes the pointer fingers on either hand down on the table edge so his hands bend in at the wrists. Melissa is probably watching me, he thinks. After eight years together it has come to this. Money. It's all there is in the end. The terrible dying baby in the hall. His chest streaked with rage. The hour before you eat. The hour before you sleep. Melissa is back there somewhere watching. She knows he's wrong. He knows he's wrong. What they need is a gas stove. That would help hydro bills. They need a vacuum cleaner. Melissa is four tables over, holding a long glass. She's holding it up in the light. There are windows lining the top of the arena walls and sunlight stands like an inverted pyramid. Melissa has managed to hold this imperfect stein into the heavy gold of the inverted apex. He thinks she looked at him, then away quickly. She is saying: Don't look at me.

Don't look at me. People are making their way to the northeast. A short man with a straw hat stands saying nothing while they move on him. He holds a black microphone wrapped in a light blue hanky. He has a cruel face and he is impatiently watching a young man rearrange boxes.

What we have here we have here we have the main event ladies and boys and boys and girls the main event here we go. We're gonna do boxes everything in the box you bid on the box and take the box the first box here we start some handy things for handy men, some tools hammer and flashlight and things you can take home and take a look…two dollars two dollars the man in suspenders three do I hear three for the box with the hammer do I have three…once it's gonna be yours ya you…once twice and that's your box for three and one the next box we have some…turn these around so I can see we have a box of canning equipment…get it all at once…the whole kit starts at two and do I hear two and two everything you need to start canning all in a box there's two the lady in the red rain coat…that's for this box here…move the box, move it… that's two two dollars come on folks that's a fine box of canning accessories going for two do I hear three three three dollars for the going once for two twice for two and sold to the lovely lady in the red...she's gonna have homemade jams and jellies...next box folks next box. What is that? What is that? Looks like a mixed box. We'll start at one buck for the mix box...one buck...anybody got a buck for this box right here...right here right here a box of mixed things... different stuff only a buck a single dollar...take a look if ya want take a look one dollar and a dollar and a dollar dollaree. Moving on...to the back here. Move! Move! Move back! We have some things from the kitchen the kitchen lotsa beauties for the kitchen and we start with the kitchen with the stove this stove it's a gas stove heats great cooks great...all the parts are there the parts the parts are all there...I used to have one just like this...self-cleaning no muss no fuss gas oven folks and in here there should be a rotisserie no siree no rotisserie that's fine we start the bid at fifty dollars fifty dollar fifty dollar fifty dollar...right there do I hear seventy-five? Seventy-five for this working gas stove she's a beaut seventy-five seventy-five seventy-five! Young man not payin' attention down here did you say seventy-five? Young man with the hand there says seventy-five go eighty go eighty go eighty. Eighty to grampa out with the grandkids wants to make thanksgiving dinner the way it wants to be...go a hundred dollars go one hundred go one hundred...this is a beaut folks...had one myself...cleans itself and heats instantaneously...one hundred...the young man with the hand... do I hear a hundred and twenty, gramps, a hundred and twenty? Mr. Hands wants it for the wife. Here she comes. Do I hear a hundred and thirty? Going once. Gramps likes the price...Mr. Hands impresses the wife. Going once going twice and sold to Mr. Hands!

Joseph's face is burnt now. It was like being on fire. The auctioneer has such hard hard eyes and he won't stop. Blow that hanky. Cough on that mic. Joseph takes a step toward his new stove and looks up. The auctioneer sees him sideways through lids that are sliding laterally across his yellow eyes. He lets him reach the oven, then points. Joseph smiles stupid and turns like a game show blonde with his hands backward to the prize. Melissa has left. He is alone now. It didn't matter what they bought here today. He was

going to be alone. Had he not bought the stove, she would still be
here. To fight one last time. Things going bad has been their theme
for a long time. She's happy now. He waits here in front of these
grim bargain hunters, feels the woolly breath of the auctioneer. The
auctioneer's a cattle man; he eases livestock through the bottleneck.
Joseph's a pigeon. A crow. A mouse lying backwards on a post. The
three older women in the front row brush the bins and sniff. A boy
in a yellow cap steals a stubby knife then chews his food. Joseph
tries to make a sad face so someone will cry, but no one does so he
drops his head back. The highest roof he has ever seen. Shooting
metal rafters and wide ribs of steel turn above him. He expects to
see the moon here, trapped and rootless, in the night sky near a nest.
It's not that he wanted Melissa to stay. It's that he knew that when
she left he would want to die. A pale red cable is woven through the
rafters in chaotic lines.

"Wanna rotisserie?"

Joseph brings his face down and the smooth floor pools around him.

"Sorry?"

"I got a rotisserie for this. Wannit?" The auctioneer's teeth are bark brown. He spits. "No charge."

"Okay."

The auctioneer blinks for a moment as if he's never laid eyes on Joseph.

"Okay."

He turns away to the boy that helps him. "I'm takin' lunch and gonna run this guy over to my place."

The kid looks at Joseph, then nods obediently to the auctioneer. The auctioneer omits details and does not like questions.

In the parking lot Joseph walks beside the auctioneer and the auctioneer doesn't seem to like this. He slows and speeds up to make Joseph look awkward doing the same. He turns abruptly down a row of parked cars and Joseph is forced to step in a puddle. He stops in front of an old red pickup. The bed is ringed by warped wood rails pulled together by heavy wire. Joseph looks back to the arena. It is small now and far away. He notices this and disapproves.

"Where's your car?"

Joseph goes to answer.

"Get in."

The door moves as if it's breaking and it closes as if it can't. The seat is a red that has faded to pink and the cab smells like uncooked meat. Joseph sits waiting. The auctioneer starts the engine.

They bounce along in silence. Joseph notices the auctioneer's hands. Swollen and dry, and the wheel glides through his palms. Such soft quiet hands. Like his throat. Pink and petal smooth.

They hit a pothole and the auctioneer's teeth clap. They are false and he must keep them loose in there.

Joseph thinks: I should put on my seat belt.

They pull up a long mud driveway but there is no house; just a wide low garage.

The auctioneer reaches down as if he's looking for a parking brake, but he brings up a tire iron. When he hits Joseph across the cheek, Joseph can see the side of his house peeking out from behind the garage. Some trees at the edge are keeping the snow on the ground. Joseph sees a purple curtain fall halfway across the windshield. The auctioneer hits his nose with something and Joseph thinks, That's right, that's how to stop me. It's not so much that Joseph is hurt; it's that the auctioneer has suddenly switched him off. Joseph's legs and arms are turning in directions without him.

Oh White Christmas! Oh Mama Mia! Oh!

102 McAllister Street

She's making an action with her hands. Old blue fingers make beak shapes and stab, biting at something imagined.

"There was none of this stuff."

Under cottony brows her eyes cross to the centre. She adds a ticking sound.

"This! This! What is *this?*"

Sam watches, thinks, "This is what makes old people so frightening; they come from outer space." Mrs. Stanley's body seizes, then loosens. She is making wide sweeps with her arms, hands tilted in an olden way of conveying elegance.

"But that was not Fay. No. Fay Wray. When the monkey saw her. Oh! Oh! He was taken, well we all were, weren't we? Fay Wray, all he had to do was, with one finger go, not dancing like this."

Mrs. Stanley does a deliberately undignified jig, bouncing her shoulders and turning her head.

"And juggling."

Her son, a large man of forty, in a brand new brown t-shirt, with his back turned. Mrs. Stanley slaps the desk, startling Sam.

"Why do all that? She's nothing. Not a thing."

Mrs. Stanley glares violently at Sam. An evil owl defiance. He gestures to the monitor in the corner of the store. Dinosaurs and an ape fighting in vines.

"Didn't have this."

Mrs. Stanley leans back, choking, clutching a thin lacey breast.

"Had it all! Had all that. This was in it."

Sam is aware that a man standing in the horror section has stopped browsing and is still.

"I guess you're right."

Her son lays a DVD box on the counter. *Hostel.* He speaks in a monotone without looking up.

"She lives in the past. Everything was better."

Mrs. Stanley backs away from the desk and seems to relax. She looks slyly from side to side as if hoping to catch someone watching.

The son stands *Hostel* on its edge so the cover faces Sam. Sam smiles in a corner of his cheek, and taps his bald head, thinking of what to say.

"Well, the first half is sex and the second half is torture."

Sam widens his face. Wideness is innocence.

Mrs. Stanley pulls the DVD case, hurting her son's hand.

"Perfect. I'll sleep through the sex and he'll sleep through the torture."

She jabs the case to her chest, chasing her breasts away.

The intersection is backed up with black trucks. Traffic lights change from orange to red without making a difference. Mother and son in a space-age white van make a left-hand turn. Sun and wind are single, blind and dry. Sprinklers toss party rice across lawns and bent crosses like plague graves hold yellow leaves and hot tomato sacs. Mrs. Stanley sits in the passenger seat with the window down. She looks for scalded children in the shadows. Little new people succumbing in the dark corners. DDT and purple foam and millions of burning pebbles. *What made us live forever,* she thinks, *fills their pointless little ears with cancer.* Her son tries to close her window.

"Hey!"

"The AC's on."

"I can't breathe with that thing on."

"It's a smog day."

You expect his voice to be whiny, but it's not. It's flat.

"Not a fuckin' smog day. It's a goddamn summer day."

She closes her paper eyelids and pushes her face out.

As they approach the driveway and slow to turn, two children teasing a tethered dog see her in the window of the van. A death's head. A skull and crossbones on the wide body of a bleach bottle. The van rolls up the driveway, tires snapping dry stones. One of the children has stepped inside the dog's reach and is bitten on the hand.

Mrs. Stanley enters the house first, backwards up grey steps, like a crab blind in tall grass. The son swings open the van's side door. He threads seven plastic bags onto his forearms. He stops for a moment and listens to the dog crying as it is struck.

Mrs. Stanley sits, disappears really, into a massive green chair. She is asleep with a remote in her hand pointed at a silent dark television. Cupboards can be heard softly opening and carefully closing. The sound of weight on linoleum. A small cough that needed to be much bigger. Then silence. The son has slipped to another part of the house while the mother sleeps. Sunlight on teacups for about an hour and a half, then as butter on the old face of an old, old clock. It thins eventually; its thinning gains some momentum near the end. Who knows what produces these effects in this ancient house? The lowering sun and ascending earth, the back of a spoon in a stand on the sill and the empty snowball tree rolling to the edge of the yard. Who knows? Late afternoons that grow later and later then, near the end, too distant to see.

She stirs when the light has gone. For a moment she thinks her husband is alive, that she has left something on the stove. She drops the remote, not seeing it, and tries to remember what she had in her hand. Far away, up in the house, footsteps. Someone big. Her husband is a small man. Light-footed. A monkey. Someone bigger is coming down. *The boy?* She can feel her heart start to bang. Something's wrong. He just turned eight last week. A yellow cake in the shape of a tire. The floor in the kitchen squawks. A man's cough. Mrs. Stanley calls out:

"Let's watch that fuckin' movie."

The son stands for a moment in the doorway, then swipes a light switch. The resulting light, a dull orange dome, makes his mad face look tired.

"What about dinner?"

"I'm not hungry."

"I mean me. For me."

Mrs. Stanley raises a hip then softly returns it. The thought of food has made her release liquid into the back of her underwear. She leans to smell herself, then clutches the couch to keep put.

The son sighs and opens the plastic DVD case.

The film begins with women baiting tourist boys by undressing.

The movie is direct with its nudity, European, and the mother and the son both watch to see how much vagina will show. One woman stares squarely into the camera, walking, unselfconscious of her large brown hair. The tiny upside-down shoulders of her vagina roll in and out of view, and if they are at all hidden it is because they point down, not because she hides them. Mrs. Stanley enjoys watching the girl's slim young sex organ rolling like dough between the twin pins of her thighs. The son is frustrated that more is not shown. It is more than usual; most films only show women's bums and tits, and even then, they are so briefly seen that they add nothing. This film shows things that are normally found in dirty movies. This overrides all else that might go on or be seen in the movie. The son wants these easy girls to lift their legs up, to pull apart their labias, to draw out into the light that final wet aperture. The son has lost interest in the movie. Wealthy men paying large sums to vivisect tourists in a filthy warehouse. It is something that doesn't happen in the real world, not like this, our fantasy of women with cocks as big as a gorilla's and vaginas opening on her, ahead of us, on her arm just before we touch it, and then, like a red stone exposed by a retreating wave, it shows on her face. Of the cocks we keep on our chest, a number spring up like planks and she uses the softer longer cocks on my hips as strings to draw me closer. Soon she is under me, her body waffled by cock dents and our mouths touch like the big balls that sway and meet between the knees of all our cock heroes. I can see them on the pillow as she surrenders, Phallic Boy with his hard orange grin. Asia Tube, Nuts Monster, and Glue Tip are warring with a witch, knocking her down with cock clubs, then crushing her warty face under the unimaginable weight of ancient ball matter.

The old woman lies on the couch while her horny son masturbates in the easy chair beside her. She knows but says nothing, doesn't look over. She grabs at her shawl as if to protect herself. This slows him for a moment, but not for long. As he orgasms, he accidentally kicks a coffee table leg and spills a glass of apple juice. Mom sits up suddenly, shrieks at him as he squeezes small tabs of semen out onto the back of his hand.

"You spilled my juice all over!"

The son has folded his hands over his penis and his thumbs are trying to drag the bottom of his shirt down.

"Don't worry! Don't worry! I'll clean it."

He sits up, his manatee body swallows his cock.

"You wanna pause the movie?"

"No. It's stupid as shit. I'm gonna clean this up and go to bed."

The son has paused the movie and is sitting forward on his long belly.

"Watch it!"

The haughty son martyrs.

"I can wait."

In the kitchen, Mrs. Stanley is suffused with rage. "He spills my drink, then pauses the movie I don't want to watch. I hate this about him. Now he'll sit in there and wait for me. That shitty movie paused and he'll sit up as if it hurts to wait."

Mrs. Stanley holds a folded linen cloth over the spill. Her son doesn't watch, but she was right, the way he sits conveys both discomfort and grand patience.

"I don't like this movie."

Mrs. Stanley's tone is softer. In spite of intensely disliking her son's pretenses, she wants to at least get along now. He picks up on this. Weakness.

"Well, you know, you were there when we rented it."

"I guess I thought you wanted to see it."

She is dabbing the cloth ineffectively. Lifting liquid, then dropping it back.

"Well, I did. But I'm not, am I?"

Mrs. Stanley looks at the screen. A man in a suit standing by a red drain.

"I'm sorry, you go ahead. I'll be quiet."

He waits before releasing the pause button, knowing that this will increase his mother's anxiety. He's right, and as the film resumes, Mrs. Stanley rattles the glass as she rights it. The noise is enough for the son to pause the movie again.

In the kitchen, Mrs. Stanley stands at the sink. She wonders who he's making her be. Could be he's like his father. Could be he's like her father. But he's not. Mrs. Stanley standing at the sink is not Mrs. Stanley sitting on the couch, either. She lifts a long thin knife from the block.

The son isn't expecting her. The sharp tip of his cock hidden sorely against his palm. He turns angrily, shaking his wet chin red, and says, "Mom, can I watch my fucking movie?"

Mrs. Stanley has tripped, but she is careless of how she might fall, only mindful that the knife go in her son somehow. It does, along his fat arm. So sharp is the knife that the end slips through his soft limb until stopped by bone. The knife stops but she falls past, her own bones weak and endangered. She pushes back up, slapping her flat fingers on the arm of his chair. His eyes are closed and he's crying, "Ow, ow, ow." She watches for a moment. Repulsed. Who cries like that when they are stabbed? You have a knife in you and the first thing you think to say is "Ow"? Mrs. Stanley finds new strength in his blubbering. She grabs the knife handle. The intensity of the tremors loosen it from bone. He wails and throws himself over, sobbing.

She drives the knife into his shoulder and he hoots loudly, straightening like a baby in a crib. His red lips are wet with snot and tears and his hands are sticky with cum. He cannot see or grab the knife. The blade slips, farting blood through his fingers. Mrs. Stanley splits the grey back of his penis and, as a tent-pole stretches a tent, the knife stretches the scrotum downward. The scrotum pops open and the imagined contents appear on Mrs. Stanley's wrist like pink leeches racing to her palm. The son vomits, but remains aware that he should express outrage.

"Mom! Stop!"

Mrs. Stanley stabs again, this time at the vomit on his stomach. She is offended by it and seeks, in jabbing repeatedly and shallow, to colanderize his soft belly, so that the vomit might fall back through. As she stabs like this, popping red corn across his torso, her son is shoving his shirt bottom low with both hands. The knife point gets caught between two hard bones on the back of his hand and, in what is probably the most painful moment, lifts a thin white straw of skeleton clear through the flesh. The son is unable to bear this and he simply passes out. He stops suddenly. The mother is on her knees, breathing heavily, the knife still screwed up into his hand. She watches his breathing for a while, the tiny bloody helicopters on his shirt swooping in closer. He is sleeping now. She wonders if he's dreaming. Do people who pass out under such circumstances dream? The cloven penis shimmies in her hand and she removes it at the base.

The movie is still on. There is probably thirty or so minutes left. It's hard to say what's happening, or even sustain interest. There is a mother on the floor, both ankles shattered and her son's penis in her hand. It's hard to pick up the film's threads. Too exhausted or excited for the movie. Movie about torture and sex might seem part of the scene, but it's not really, not with the mother's head low and snoring and the cock socket draining the fat body away. The carpet edge. The slipper bent in half, soaking. The "this kind of thing happens all the time" rumble of the sump pump from below. Happens all the time. Lying on your back nearby, a phone cord between your toes and the smell of those two. So many Americans are fucked up. Lost. Hiding in alligators. Pregnant with filler. Moss hangs off them. Yellow teeth and eyes. The curtains here hang heavy, unmoving. Purple. There are lots of people no smarter than dogs.

102 McAllister Street

At this time of year, late summer, Main Street lines up with the rising sun's rays. Through the gold air walks ten-year-old Lisa. Her red hair hangs in front of her face. She has Fetal Alcohol Syndrome. She would seem rude if you asked her the time. There is a smile on her small red lips. She turns at a sculpture of a Victorian man and woman. It is the Horticulture Society's Memorial to Innocent Victims of Abortion. She has a parasol and he, a tall hat. Some of the stones in the base garden have been loosened deliberately and lie on the path. Lisa steps through them and across Elm to Hickory. Hickory has a sidewalk and is shaded at this time of day and she continues along, even though Elm would be more sensible. Russian sunflowers are lawn monsters in late August. None of the crisp lighter green or sharp citrus colours of spring. Gardens and lawns are plant-gory from protracted sexual wars. Lisa comes to the end of the sidewalk and walks along the edge of sodden ditches that foot properties. She sees something out of the edge of her view. A sleeping dog on bare ground. A policeman sitting on the steps of a side porch. Lisa slows to look. This is Mrs. Stanley's house. She cannot resist the impulse to march up the driveway. If her mother hadn't drank continuously throughout the pregnancy then Lisa could have minded her own business. Instead, she approaches the officer.

Officer Shelley turns his rock face to the girl. She is reflected in his mirror shades as an older, thinner woman who bows through the middle.

"Hello, young lady."

Lisa stops, puts a hand over her eyes and settles all her weight on her left side. She stares down at Shelley. The officer grows uncomfortable, which is something Lisa intends or is entirely oblivious to—either way, her mother should not have kept drinking.

"Something I can help you with?"

Lisa balances her weight for a moment, suggesting that she might make a turn, but brings herself down on the right.

"Somethin' smells off. What's that shitty smell?"

Shelley lowers his head and points his heavy boot under a stick.

"You wouldn't believe me if I told you."

Lisa sees something. A little pattern of wretch sinking into the dirt.

"What that? That what stinks?"

"Nope. That, little lady, is where I just had a puke."

"How come?"

"Isn't there somewhere you need to be?"

"How come you sicked up?"

"Dead bodies."

Shelley gestures with a thrown thumb.

"In there."

Lisa looks at the closed door and makes a thinking sneer.

"So. Haven't you ever smelled dead bodies before? You're a cop."

"Yes, Miss. I have. But what's in there is..."

Shelley stops. His sinuses are filling up. He sniffs hard.

"Are you crying?"

"No. I'm not crying."

"Shouldn't you be catching out whoever did this, instead of crying all over?"

"I ain't cryin', I got...my nose is bothered."

"So what's in there?"

Shelley is annoyed now and wants to scare her. He pulls his glasses down his nose so she can see his big honest eyes.

"There's a man in there all cut open by a knife."

"So."

"Yeah, so. And his wiener cut clean off."

"His wiener?"

"That's what I said."

"So. I know somebody who needs to have that done."

"By his own mom?"

"His mom cut off his wiener?"

"She's dead, too. Lying right beside him with his dead wiener in her hand. And it's cut in two right down the middle like a goddamn hot dog."

"Is that what smells?"

"Yes, ma'am. That and seeing as to the fact that they shit themselves."

"How come?"

"How come what?"

"How come they shit themselves?"

Shelley runs a pen down the blue piping on the side of his knee. He clicks it, retracting the ballpoint.

"Because, that is what you do."

The Rabbit Place

Belle and Cor examine the map of Italy on a placemat.

"How big are whales?"

A whale with a sunny smile and a jaunty plume sits off the toe. Belle knows that Cor is trying to gauge the size of things on the map. If the whale is a mile long, then it is about four miles from Roma to Milano. Cor's first instinct is to trust what he sees, then try to understand it. Belle smiles. She has no idea how big the boot is, but she knows that there is no way to tell by looking at this drawing.

"Whales are bigger than any animal. Ever."

Cor studies the map again. "Where's Duntroon?"

Belle tosses her hair back with both hands. She's about to settle for Cor the impossibility of knowing everything when, as she often does, she decides that Cor's onto something.

Belle pulls the paper cup of crayons over and starts to draw lines across Italy.

"What's that s'posed to be?"

Belle takes a stubby pencil and writes Sydenham Trail. Erie Street. In a heavy cross in the middle she writes 124 and 91.

"Now. It's a map of Duntroon."

"Write that."

Belle writes DUNTROON in big blocks across the word Italy. Making the I an N, the T a bolder T, the A an R, the L an O. The best she can to with the Y is a Q. Cor sees this and can now accept that it is a map of Duntroon.

"Now we have to put stuff from Duntroon on it. We don't have whales."

Cor looks at her as if she's crazy, then puts thinking fingers under each eye.

"Like what?"

"I dunno."

"Raccoons?"

Belle looks out the tall window beside their table. Cor watches her do this, then lays his head down. A heavy truck hammers past. A small red car. Blue. A long white truck with a milk logo. Belle sits back as if stung. She points without pointing. Cor turns his head on his arm, then sits up quickly.

Whispered: Poo Lady.

Poo Lady appears once a day in Duntroon. She pushes an old-fashioned light blue baby carriage and wears a green housecoat. She has curlers in her hair. Local children believe she rolls poo that she finds in the park, and maybe even her own, into her hair. They also believe that there is a baby made of poo bouncing around in the pram. There is a literal aura around this woman, a fecal spell, and it is believed that if you even say her name, Poo Lady, or, God forbid, ever spoke to her that your breath would smell of farts for the rest of your life. Everything about her, the colour of green, the thin black wheels, the filthy fart cigarette in her mouth, had done something unspeakable to someone at some point. The worst part of her is the lie, the horrible pushing as if the baby were in there. Belle and Cor shudder. She has passed the window.

"Put the (whispered) Poo Lady on the map."

Belle sighs. She suffers for having a younger brother. Cor's forehead lands hard on the back of his hands and stays.

"Okay. Okay. I know. I know exactly. We'll do the weird map of Duntroon. All the things that are here that no one talks about. All the stuff *we* know about."

Cor sits up.

"Poo Lady?"

"Poo Lady."

And so they begin to make their map starting with a colour-true drawing of the Poo Lady on the 124. She is encircled in light brown. Then there is the House of Cruelty at the end of Erie Street. A pilot lives there who has gone mad because he spends more time in the sky than on the ground. The only way he can keep from killing children is to drown cats in a barrel in his back yard. Then there is the Stab Forest. A heavy tangle of thorn trees down the hill behind the legion on the west route out of town. The body of a woman was found in there five years ago. Her husband was taken away, but the children know it was the spikes that got her. Piercing through her clothes and literally pulling out her heart and flinging it to the ground. Then on Sydenham, the Cherry House. In it lives a giant woman and her daughter who is grown up but only as tall as a two-year-old. This woman sings songs to God under her breath and the daughter cackles and twists when she walks. Half of her body never came out of her mother, is still growing inside somewhere, tightening the old woman's shoulders. The mother is in so much pain that she sings to God under her breath every second of every day. The daughter is a kind of devil.

Belle and Cor sit silently for a long while trying to think of other things to put on the map.

"The fishing hole."

"That's not weird."

"All the grade sixers pee in it on their way home from school."

"So? That's just gross."

"Yeah. But nobody knows. Might be good to tell them."

Belle makes a blue circle and fills it with yellow. Gross alone is too low a standard, but gross and *informative* isn't.

Belle and Cor stand on the narrow walkway at the side of their house. Belle turns and faces the heavy ivy. She lifts the back of her shirt and instructs her brother to press the map against her bare back then pull the shirt over it.

"Mom and Dad don't need to know about this."

She instructs Cor to hurry. Wasps are emerging from the shadows beneath the leaves. She closes her eyes until he is done.

That night Belle lies awake in her bed. The map lies in the dust beneath her box spring. She is waiting, as she does every night, for her fear to rise before falling asleep. She has to select what the fear can rise into safely. Usually a sound or rather the space between two sounds. The ductwork snaps somewhere in the house. Too alert, too random to make a proper space. A pump scrolls through water in the basement. Across the hall, Cor coughs. Cor is coughing in his sleep. Then she finds it. The electric clock groans and ticks and then is silent. Not silent really, more suspended until the next groan and tick. *That* is the space. Belle focuses on the space. She needs to be accurate or the fear will never come and she will never sleep. The space is a hole. A gap. A non-groan and a non-tick. It is a thing covered or a thing removed. She races around it trying to make it what it is. It is a groan breathing in instead of out. It is all the silent ticks awaiting selection. Belle feels her ears grow larger than her pillow. It is the thinking about groaning and the remembering about ticking. Her eyes reach down and draw heavy bedding up into her thoughts. Belle feels her heart start to plink in the space. It is dying. The space between the groan and the tick is dying. Belle's hands release around the bear at her chest and she falls to sleep.

Belle checks that Cor's shoes are on the right feet. He stands looking up at her, waiting. She nods.

"Do you have the map?"

Belle nods.

"I gave it a title. It needs to be called something."

Cor grabs his cheeks, agreeing.

"What is it called? What? What?"

"*Shhhh.* Outside."

Belle looks back into the house as the storm door slaps closed behind Cor.

Cor waits outside, standing in a puddle. He feels dirty water wick up his instep. Belle emerges and carefully turns to close the door. She points to the end of the driveway then follows her brother, avoiding the puddle and stepping between the faint shades of his wet footprints.

"Keep going. Don't act weird."

The end of Erie Street and stop. Duntroon sits on top of the Niagara Escarpment and from there you can see all of Clearview Township. From Creemore out to Cashtown. The steeples of Stayner and the entire Nottawasaga Bay including the beaches of Tiny Township. The view is sweeping and the perspective so odd that it translates to your eye like wallpaper in a Chinese restaurant.

Belle turns her back and casts a quick shadow, her head darkens the centre of Christian Island some eighty kilometres away. She carefully rolls up the back of her shirt and Cor draws the map off her skin.

"It's called The Evil Tour of Duntroon."

Cor closes an eye to think. Belle watches.

"Anyway, that's what it is."

Cor's face falls.

"It's mine too. I thought it."

Belle remembers.

"Okay. Okay. What do you think? The Evil Tour of Duntroon."

Cor closes the eye again and Belle patiently looks at her map.

"What about Giant Scorpion Attacks?"

"What about *what?*"

"Giant Scorpion Attacks."

Belle controls herself. Cor holds his chin and stares at the map. He is the decider.

"Okay. We go with your one. What was it again?"

"The Evil Tour of Duntroon."

Belle pulls out a drawing pencil and begins to write the title in block letters at the top.

Neither child is aware that a man has approached. He has come down from the crest of the high street and is stopped, stooped over them as Belle finishes.

"The Evil Tour of Duntroon."

The children jump towards each other as if to pounce on the words written that they have just heard spoken.

The man laughs and pulls his hat back off his face.

"Don't worry! Don't worry. The secret's safe. Is it a secret?"

Belle is too upset to speak. Cor grins and nods. He believes the map's importance has now begun.

"Can I see your map?"

The man's hand falls open against Belle's arm. She knows him. She has seen him. Not his name, but him. He sits on the stool beside the antique tractors at the fair in October. He sits beside a barrel fire with a yellow dog resting by his feet. At the fair his hat is light-coloured. He holds the map up close to his face and studies it.

"The Poo Lady. Hmmm."

Belle feels fire move around her throat. Cor claps both hands to his mouth. He's too nervous to actually laugh, but he thinks this could be funny.

"Astounding. I didn't know children could still see her."

Belle looks at his face. He is serious. She dislikes being patronized and can tell quickly when that's happening.

"It's an impressive tour. I will never tell a soul. You have my word."

He reaches his hand out and after a pause Belle takes it and they shake once, firmly. The man looks slightly nervous. Surprised.

"I look forward to seeing it completed."

He bows and turns. Cor is suddenly overcome with the sensation that the police will come. He repeats his phone number and address carefully in his head. Belle calls after the man.

"But it is. It is done."

The man stops and pauses before turning around. He looks at the children and slowly removes his hat. A long strip of grey wires spring up off his head and point away from the bay. He takes a step towards them and stops.

"Okay. You're done then. It's a terrific map."

Belle walks up to him before he can turn to go.

"No, it's not. It's not done. Is it?"

The man looks down at the girl. His eyes are wide. She has caught him at something.

"Why isn't it done?"

For a moment she thinks the man is going to cry, but breathes deep, accepting a responsibility, and leans in close to speak. There's something too grown up about him now. Belle regrets her question.

"If your map is complete you must include the rabbit place behind the community centre."

Belle blinks and looks down at her map. *Rabbit place?*

"When we were kids the family raised rabbits there. It's right there."

His finger stabs at the map. Belle looks back to check for Cor. He hasn't moved.

"Why should I? What's weird about that place?"

"Evil. Your map *is* the evil tour. This spot. This place is."

"Is what?"

"Is evil."

The man scans the street around him, looks out into the bay.

"Just don't go there. Just put it on your map."

"I *will* go there."

"I said don't. You listen to me."

"Then tell me what's there."

The man might yell. He's drawing himself up to yell.

"Please, Mister."

His shoulders fall in as if something substantial has just escaped from him. He pushes his mouth hard into the back of his hand then speaks in a long single breath.

"I didn't see it myself. Not well. I did see it. There's a head on the couch at the top of the stairs."

He glares, wanting this to sink in. Belle takes a step back.

"There's a what on a what?"

"A head on a couch. I saw it from halfway up the stairs and that day, three of my friends who did get to the top never came back down."

"What happened?"

"I ran away before I could see. They just…they were missing from that moment on. Other kids too. That summer and the next."

Cor is now beside Belle. He asks her instead of the man.

"What kind of head?"

The man closes his eyes tightly.

"An old woman's head, I think. There was no body."

Again to his sister.

"Was she dead?"

The man uses his hand to stop from laughing.

"Actually, no. She wasn't. It was yelling from the couch."

The man takes a deep shivery breath, wipes his face, then stands straight. He is looking down now and Belle can tell that he's finished playing this game, whatever it is.

"And so, that's that. I told you and that's that. Put it in your map or don't."

Belle feels sharply that there is real meanness in this story. She knows that when strangers try to scare children very bad things are involved.

Belle and Cor watch the man walking quickly down the hill to the long road that rolls over farmland to Stayner. From that moment on Belle stopped hiding the map. She wasn't sure what had happened to it, but was aware that it had lost something. It had lost its pull. It was something that adults do. They have no sense of proportion, of size. It wasn't that he was trying to lure the children into a derelict building; to Belle, that was garden variety grown-up shenanigans and not her problem. Her problem was that the map had been deformed. An old woman's head on a couch that somehow removed children from the world. This is more than just a lie. It forced everything else on the map to be true and she wasn't sure, now that the map had lost its voice, that these things were true. The half-baby growing inside the mother. The cherry tree tearing out the lady's heart. None of it stays together if it isn't said in a certain way by certain people at a certain time. Belle pictures the whale smiling as it rests on the water by the Italian toe. It is its second nature that is sunny and insane and probably twenty miles long.

Belle and Cor play in the park until lunchtime. They don't speak of the map again. They pretend they are apes for a while, then they walk on the moon and then, and she doesn't know how or why, they pretend to steal straw from the baby Jesus's manger. At home Belle lays the map on the counter for her mom to find. It will end up on the fridge beside drawings of her stick family beneath the sun.

Cor scoops up his tomato soup in a spoon too big for his mouth. Belle thinks he's no smarter than a dog. She's aware that this is another effect of the ruined map. She blows on her soup until it cools, then pushes it away.

"I'm going to my room."

Cor turns his heavy spoon and the rash-coloured soup drops to the table. He is a puppy standing in its water dish. Belle leaves him.

She lies on her bed for an hour looking up at the glow in the dark stars on her ceiling. The room is sunny so the stars are taking light and not giving it. In time she becomes aware of an odd sensation. A shift in the sunlight. A cloud probably passed over the sun, but it triggers a mild panic in her. Belle sits up on the edge of her bed. Her shadow waves across the floor as if time has sped up. Something is wrong.

The map is gone. Belle slaps her hand on the counter where she left it.

"Cor?"

She calls from the middle of the room.

"Cor?"

From the middle of the house.

"Cor?"

From the middle of the yard.

"Cor!"

The top of the street.

"Cor!"

Oh no, he didn't. He didn't. He didn't.

Belle dashes to the end of Erie Street and runs through the intersection below the community hall. Gravel trucks and seagulls shred the sky around her. A row of rusted barrels hold back the cherry trees in the alley. A bathtub sits on bare dirt. A Christmas decoration. Rudolph. Santa.

The house is a frightening face, dark and grinning, but Belle doesn't notice this as she leaps across the porch and trips through the screen door.

"Cor!"

A stove in the middle of the sitting room to the right.

"Cor!"

A pigeon in the kitchen. A pigeon!

"Cor!"

Belle stands at the bottom of the stairs. She can't see the top but knows this is where it happens. Each step is bowed and worn smooth as a shin. Halfway up she can see the top of the couch. Then the arm rests. It sits against the wall below a painting of a boathouse. The cushions are heavy and settled deep and empty. No old lady's head. No head.

"Cor!"

Belle stands for a moment listening to silence and leaning in the mote-pricked sunlight at the top of the stairs. A sharp pencil of light. Another. Belle raises her hands, unsure of what she sees. Tiny holes are opening in the wall and sending white beams of sunlight across her path. They make a cat's cradle of daylight pulled tight from wall to wall. Belle instinctively steps back from where she thinks the next one will appear. And it does. Bullets. Bullets are popping in through the walls. She turns and runs down the stairs. Cor lies on the lawn in the backyard beside the man.

She skids across the ground. Nothing can stop her. She is fleeing death. A monster is screaming at her.

At the end of the alley she tries to stop. But she is too late and she slams into the side of a pale blue pram and tumbles through its upended wheels. A gravel truck grinds its brakes into the clouds and a long white pupa unravels under Belle. The baby's face is twisted in a cry and it is rust and yellow with spidery veins breaking on its cheeks. The baby throws a small hand up that falls off. Dung bones separate from dung flesh as a thousand curls of fetid air become unbreathable clumps of light.

Fairground Road

The world is a place of mighty lights. Huge things collect on us, around our voices in hurried shapes and on the outline of our actions. We see things, giant things, and quickly we claim them—wars are particularly ours, but so are pandemics and the influence of falling things on newspaper hats. Lost to us, in that white noise, are the millions of moments, unlike singular wars, which happen, then hurry from the stage, hardly ever lasting beyond the breath it takes to say they're here and are so monumentally shattering that we would break from reality to cope.

In a small village in China a child is found alive in the bowels of a trout. There is a pond on a farm on the brink of the Amazon that is so full of paint thinners that a faint flame lives in the air above it. There are people born without legs. With four legs. With beaks and sticks and ten eyes and goat bellies and humpback chub eyes and mouthless and earless with brains exposed to winter wind and hands not there that pull on a strange mother turning away and unzipped bowels with chattering teeth and fin tongues and gill lungs and hundreds of tiny eyes and hundreds of tiny feet and thousands of tiny mouths and these things, these part words that never rise to any level, are seething and happy that we will all die with them. We will all die with them.

Jason is standing on the east side of Fairground Road walking north. It is why they call this part of the country Clearview. Wide meadows reaching into farm fields that lift slowly at first, then trot up quickly onto the knees of Blue Mountain. He can see a great distance from the side of the road. Crumbling black barns and long stitchy lines pull and follow the land like details on an old sweater. The oldest movement of sky and earth are visible here—the clouds tear on the escarpment's razor with the same sound they have made for millions of years. Silence is what it is, but it sounds like somewhere in all these giant brown and green tumblers a terrible ripping is deafening the ground.

Jason has seen things here, postage stamp things. The Collingwood Horse Show where the Olympic team, headed by the silly face of Captain Canada, rolls around on hard brown-and-black horses, bounding over Saabs and Peugeots. A long summer afternoon with rich children sitting on collapsible chairs while thin uncles and ropey moms scrub million-dollar beasts. When the clouds are canker white and the ash trees are green and the sun is a minute old, there is nothing as perfect as being here with tan pants on.

Jason remembers the summer before last, he and Liz made their way back from the final jump. An improbably short pear-shaped girl had won. Jason was tempted to think that the rich can afford not to look sporty in their sport. Liz spotted something. A round little boy running towards them with arms waving. A magical panic balloon bounced towards them between the highest sky and the brown irregular lines vanishing under him to the horizon.

"Mister! Help! Mister!"

Liz stopped. She looked back: Well, Mister?

Jason jumped forward, feeling odd to be running toward a boy in a painting like this. The boy was crying and red; his friend, he said, was stuck in the mud. Jason walked with him along the wet ditch as the boy sucked slobber back between his scarlet lips.

Now that Jason is standing here, across the road from where this happened, it can't be recalled without raising the dead of a year ago. He stops for a moment and tries to picture everything that stands between the two summers. The summer of the child in the ditch and the summer of hundreds dead. In this field. Some shot to be buried. Some families like long worms spilling from a paper carton into the earth. It's an old story, the lining of things with children, but it was new here, in this fairground, abandoned now, abandoned but for Jason and his little string of memories of the boy's friend stuck up to his knees in fine sucking silt. We killed them all, didn't we? In our madness and our fear we tore through ourselves to get somewhere better, maybe to get to here, to now. Jason's standing on the soft graves of last summer, remembering the saved horse trader's son, crying out from the mud, "Don't tell my mommy!"

Jason and Liz had a better day after that. He had proven he could save children.

The bumpy little road is still here and the low fences cordoning off acres. During the Great Northern Exhibition there are Ferris wheels and cotton candy stands. Massive bulls and prize chickens. A skinny man with long grey hair runs a squalid little petting corral. The skinny man sells green pellets in orange cones from a dented metal dish. He winks at the children who touch his short, hard-cheeked pigs. He grins at parents, a pot smoker's grin, and refers to children as "the little ones…"

There is an orange-and-red SUV up ahead parked in the middle of the field. A man is sitting on a metal chest while another stands examining a large camera. Jason lowers his head and continues walking. There is smoke rising from a chimney near the base of Blue Mountain. Jason kicks something and stops. Four blue cylinders. Shotgun shells. They were supposed to have completely cleaned this ground. He bends down and picks them up. They must be new. Things that happened so long ago don't glow in blue plastic. War crimes aren't toadstools. Somebody shooting birds. Squirrels. Probably not fired into the backs of captives.

"Excuse me, sir?"

The two guys have run over to Jason. He drops the shells.

"Hi."

"Hey, what brings you to the fairgrounds?"

Jason is not normal any more so he kills them.

« THE END »

Acknowledgements

Thanks to the folks at Anvil—Brian, Karen, & Aimee

Rachel let-the-right-one-in Jones

Griffin and Camille for listening

 TONY BURGESS is the author of *The Hellmouths of Bewdley*, *Pontypool Changes Everything*, *Caesarea*, and *Fiction For Lovers*. His writing has been featured in numerous anthologies and magazines across the country. Most recently, Tony was nominated for a Genie Award for Best Adapted Screenplay for *Pontypool*. He lives in Stayner, Ontario.